Flash Digest

April 2024

Edited by
Tyree Campbell
& Terrie Leigh Relf

THE STAFF OF FLASH DIGEST

EDITORS: Tyree Campbell & Terrie Leigh Relf
WEBMASTER: H. David Blalock
COVER DESIGNERS: Laura Givens; Marcia A. Borell

Cover art by Jade Sng
Cover design by Laura Givens

Vol. I, No.1   April 2024

Flash Digest is published four times a year on the 1st days of January, April, July, and October in the United States of America by Hiraeth Publishing, P.O. Box 1248, Tularosa, NM, 88352. Copyright 2024 by Hiraeth Publishing. All rights revert to authors and artists upon publication except as noted in selected individual contracts. Nothing may be reproduced in whole or in part without written permission from the authors and artists. Any similarity between places and persons mentioned in the fiction or semi-fiction and real places or persons living or dead is coincidental. Writers and artists guidelines are available online at www.hiraethsffh.com. Guidelines are also available upon request from Hiraeth Publishing, P.O. Box 1248, Tularosa, NM, 88352, if request is accompanied by a self-addressed #10 envelope with a first-class US stamp.

Contents

11   Wildflower Ghost by Maureen Bowden

20   A Change in the Contract by Glenis Moore

22   Where Did All the Fairy Tale Creatures Go by Gary Davis

26   End of Term by Matias Travieso-Diaz

30   Is There a Sign I Should Know by Tyree Campbell

34   Woman in the Moon by Terrie Leigh Relf

**THERE'S A SALE GOING ON!!!
IT'S STILL GOING ON!!!**

BUY ALL THE BOOKS YOU WANT AND USE THIS 20% DISCOUNT CODE: BOOKS2024

THIS DISCOUNT CAN BE USED AS MANY TIMES AS YOU WISH, SO TAKE ADVANTAGE OF IT!

GO TO OUR SHOP AT WWW.HIRAETHSFFH.COM

NO MASKS, NO WAITING, AND WE NEVER CLOSE!

A Little Help, Please

In the world of the small indie press we fight a never-ending battle for attention to our work, as writers and in publishing. Here's an example: big publishers [you know who they are] have gobs of $$$ that they can devote to advertising and marketing. Here at Hiraeth Publishing, our advertising budget consists of the deposits for whatever soda bottles and aluminum cans we can find alongside the highways. Anti-littering laws make our task even more difficult . . . ☺

That's where YOU come in. YOU are our best promoter. YOU are the one who can tell others about us. Just send 'em to our website, tell them about our store. That's all. Just that.

Of course, we don't mind if you talk us up. We're pretty good, you know. We have some award-winning and award-nominated writers and artists, plus other voices well-deserving to be heard [not everyone wins awards, right?] but our publications are read-worthy nevertheless.

That number once again is:

www.hiraethsffh.com

Friend us on Facebook at Hiraeth Publishing
Follow us on Twitter at @HiraethPublish1

The Saint and the Demon

By t.santitoro & Ron Sparks

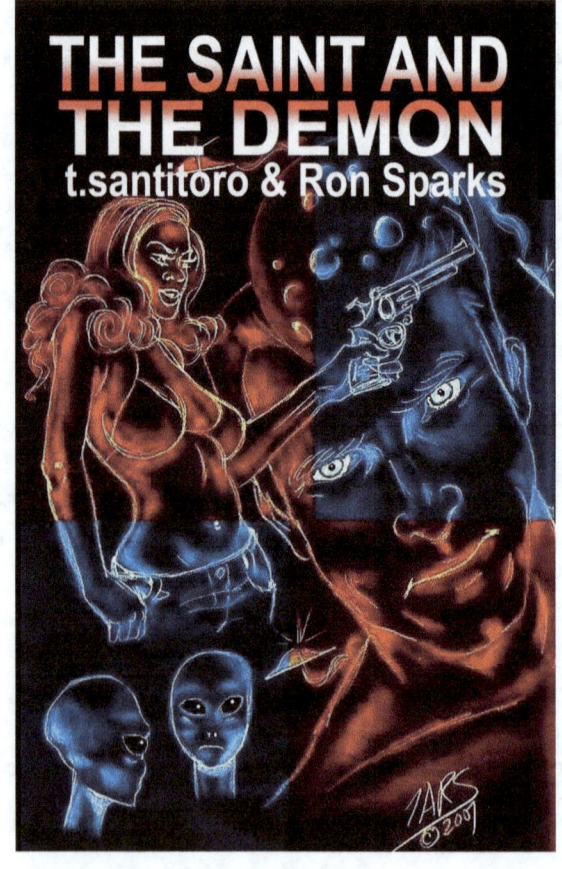

In the not-to-distant future, a young reporter reluctantly agrees to interview a senile old man in the heart of the Florida Everglades. In the humid, swampy environment, the reporter is sure that there can be no story of substance here, but the old man reveals that, in the past, his love was so strong and so passionate for a woman that he stopped at nothing to get her back when the forces of war tore them apart. He became a hero and a coward, a lover and a fighter . . . a saint and a devil. In his quest to rescue the woman he loved, he became something that she could no longer love.

Into the middle of this personal ordeal tumbles Cutter, a man from another world, sent to Earth to establish a breeding mission for his endangered race. He falls in love with an Earth woman, and must defend not only her, but also the future of his own people. The object of his alien affections, an innocent young woman named Angel, finds herself suddenly thrust into a world of aliens and intrigue, and of a love that has far more dangerous consequences than she could possibly have imagined.

Type: Novel – science fiction

Ordering Link:
Print ($13.95): https://www.hiraethsffh.com/product-page/saint-and-the-demon-by-t-santitoro-and-ron-sparks
PDF ($4.99): https://www.hiraethsffh.com/product-page/saint-the-demon-by-t-santitoro-ron-sparks
ePub ($4.99): https://www.hiraethsffh.com/product-page/saint-amp-the-demon-by-t-santitoro-amp-ron-sparks

The Gifted
By Tyree Campbell

DEDICATED TO THE
MEMORY OF MELISSA MEAD

The year is 2045. Earth's societies have fallen apart for various reasons—economic, social, political, disease. To live, people began to loot, kill each other, and generally get by from day to day. In the latter stages of this deterioration, fear of disease caused immunizations to be rushed into production without proper testing. Some parents soon discovered that the children born were deformed in some way: flippers for hands and/or feet, missing organs, scales for skin, etc.

In addition to flippered hands and feet, Wendy Meade was gifted with some psi abilities that enabled her to talk with animals and with people. Now an adult woman, she scrapes by in a woods above a bay on the coast of southern Oregon, where there is an abandoned town where food is still available in convenience stores. She supplements this with shellfish from the bay. Such is her life.

Until one day she discovers that she can telepath with animals and people. A small community begins to form around her. Now, if possible, she has to use her powers to protect them from marauders.

Type: Post-Apocalyptic Novel
Cover price: Print: $14.95; ePub: $3.99; PDF: $3.99
Ordering links:
Print: https://www.hiraethsffh.com/product-page/gifted-by-tyree-campbell
ePub: https://www.hiraethsffh.com/product-page/gifted-by-tyree-campbell-1
PDF: https://www.hiraethsffh.com/product-page/gifted-by-tyree-campbell-2

Tales From the Quantum Café
by Alan Ira Gordon

A collection of oddments created over lunch—you'll find them in this volume. There's an homage to the Thimble Theater; a treatment of the Revolutionary War in terms of a baseball game; small-town environmental problems; a random pun here and there; life on the Outback; the secret of the Drake equation; an off-beat look at Disney; and much, much more!

https://www.hiraethsffh.com/product-page/tales-from-the-quantum-cafe-by-alan-ira-gordon

Wildflower Ghost
Maureen Bowden

Joannie Deegan sat on the high wall overlooking Edge Hill Station railway line. She was crying. "Where are you, Robbie?" She called. "Don't be frightened. I'll wait for you." She heard nothing but the sound of rain splashing into the gutters along Tunnel Road. Climbing to her feet, she looked across the empty platform. The wind whipped her dress around her legs and blew her hair into her eyes. She missed her footing on the wall's wet stones, and fell.

The evening train from Birmingham to Liverpool Lime Street steamed into Edge Hill Station. No passengers were alighting or boarding. There was no need for the train to stop. The driver saw the child lying on the track. He braked, but it was too late.

* * *

Joannie wandered around the station for sixty years, waiting for Robbie. When people spotted her they shuddered and fled, except the man with the kind face. He smiled and waved. She thought maybe she should ask him if he'd seen Robbie, but next time she saw him there was a girl, about her age, with him. Joannie's courage failed and she kept out of sight.

* * *

My grandfather and I sat on the grassy railway embankment at Edge Hill Station, feeding the pigeons that roosted on the ticket office and waiting-room roofs. They perched upon his shoulder and hopped onto his hand to take stale bread and broken biscuits. He taught me how to call them as we held out our food-filled palms. Tiny pointed claws balanced on our wrists, making indentations in our skin.

We walked beside the grime-caked railway wall where dandelions grew in the dirt. Little kids tittered behind their hands, calling them 'Pee-the-Beds'.

"Let's give them a posh name," I said. "Like Edge Hill Marigolds?"

He nodded. "If you say so, Lindy. Edge Hill Marigolds it is."

We watched the white steam rising from the trains thundering under Tunnel Road, and I said, "Tell me about the ghost, Granddad." I'd heard the story a thousand times, but although it scared me I never tired of it.

"Her name was Joan Deegan," he said. "About your age, she was. Sixty years ago she fell onto the track and a train hit her."

"Have you ever seen her?"

"Aye, lass. Lots of people have. Sometimes she sits on the wall. At other times she wanders around looking lost. It seems like she's searching for someone."

I shivered, and noticed that some of the dandelions were dead: their golden petals replaced by a seed head, a wildflower ghost that the kids called a daddy bunchy. They'd make a wish as they blew the seeds into the wind.

I reached for Granddad's hand. The early evening light defined the contours of his face, in the last slow rolling hour before dusk.

He died the day after my eleventh birthday. The world changed, and became a darker place. My family said I was too young to go to the funeral but after it was over I picked a handful of Edge Hill Marigolds, wrapped them in a paper tissue shroud, carried them to his grave, and placed them between the proud, grown-up flowers.

I lay in bed that night, listening to cats keening and dogs barking in the backyards; a plane's drone overhead, recalling my parents' tales of the Blitz; the foghorns on the tugs as city smog descended upon the River Mersey. Through my bedroom window's drawn-back curtains, I saw the chimneystacks that looked like old men with their flat caps, sitting on the opposite rooftops, as they had every night I could remember. The damp stains on my bedroom ceiling were old friends: legacies of the landlord-neglected roof. I picked out the two-headed cat, the lopsided crinoline lady with her high headdress, and the mighty wizard, Merlin, with his pointed hat and billowing cloak. In the blurred edges of the newest stain I thought I could detect the outline of Granddad's face. Pulling the covers over my head I cried myself to sleep.

I dreamed of him. He spoke to me, "Lindy, we have to help Joan. Ask her who she's looking for."

"But she's a ghost. I'm frightened of ghosts."

"You're not frightened of me, are you?"

"Of course not. I know you. You're a real person."

"So is Joan. She's a lonely little girl. We have to find out what's keeping her here. You must ask her."

"But I've never even seen her, and why would she tell me?"

"Because she could do with a friend."

"So could I. You shouldn't have died, Granddad. I miss you." I tried to hold his hand, but it remained out of reach.

"I know, lass," he said, "but don't you worry, the sadness will pass and you'll be ship-shape and ready to live your life, just as I did."

"Then I'll die, and that scares me."

"There's nothing to be scared about," he said. "When our time comes we have to go. Joan can't. She's stuck. That's why she needs our help."

It was months before I could face going anywhere near the station: not only because Joan's ghost might be there, but mostly because Granddad wouldn't. I thought about him all the time. My parents kept an album of family photographs on the top shelf of their wardrobe. I stood on a chair to reach it, stole the photos of granddad, and hid them, with my other treasures, in the old blue desk beside my bed. He would have said it was wrong to do that, but like the railway ghost, I was stuck.

I dreamed of Granddad often. It was always the same dream. He kept telling me I had to help Joan. A year after his death, I found the courage to walk along Tunnel Road. A little girl was sitting on the high wall that overlooked the railway line. I called to her, "It's dangerous up there. You'll fall."

She giggled, "I already did."

I shivered, but felt relieved that now I was facing her she wasn't so scary. "Is your name Joan?" I said.

"Yes, but I'm called Joannie. What's your name?"

"Belinda. You can call me Lindy."

"Where's the man?"

"Which man?"

"The one who comes here with you. He has a kind face, like the king's picture on pennies."

I felt the sharp pain of Granddad's absence. "He's gone."

"Where?"

"Wherever people go when they die."

"That's where I should go, isn't it?"

"Yes. Why are you still here?"

"I'm waiting for Robbie." Her voice trembled. "Have you seen him?"

I shook my head. "No."

Her shoulders slumped, and she rubbed the heel of her hand across her eyes.

I sat on the ground and leaned against the railway wall. "Come down and tell me about Robbie."

She sat beside me. "He's my little brother. I took care of him. That was my job because Mam had six others, so she had enough to do." She stopped, and looked around. "This was our favourite place. I used to bring him to see the trains. He must be here somewhere."

"What happened to him, Joannie?" I said.

"He caught scarlet fever and died when he was only three. I know he'll come to meet me, and if I've gone he'll be frightened, so I have to wait for him." She was faded and fragile as a daddy bunchy, refusing to be blown and scattered by the wind.

I didn't know what to do, but Granddad might know. "I'll try to help," I said. "I'll talk to the man. Maybe he can find Robbie." Being close to her made me feel cold and sad. I pulled myself to my feet. "I must go home now."

"She called to me as I walked away, "Thank you, Lindy." I looked back but she'd gone.

That night I dreamed of Granddad again, and I told him about Robbie. "Can you find him?" I asked.

"If he wants to be found, I will. You've done well, Lindy. Go to the station again tomorrow."

In the early evening I walked alongside the railway wall, and raised my hand to shade my eyes from the setting sun. Three figures were silhouetted against the blue and gold sky: Joannie, a small boy, and Granddad. They waved goodbye, and then they vanished.

Before I went to bed that night I took the stolen photos out of my desk and replaced them in my parents' album. Joannie and I had both found peace.

*   *   *

That was a lifetime ago. Today I visited my childhood neighbourhood, and I walked, once again, past the now derelict station. Steam engines are a distant memory and even modern trains don't stop here now. The ticket office and the waiting-room are abandoned and crumbling. The pigeons have gone too, but Edge Hill Marigolds still grow in the city dirt. I picked a daddy bunchy, cradled the sad little wildflower ghost in my hand, made a wish, and blew the seeds into the wind.

Whispers of Magic
By Maureen Bowden

Legends and unusual characters abound in England, where you never know who or what you might meet in the forests. Maureen Bowden introduces you to them in these stories of magic and misdirection…and invites you to stay.

Maureen Bowden is a Liverpudlian, living with her musician husband in North Wales. In addition to stories, she also writes song lyrics, mostly comic political satire, set to traditional melodies. She loves her family and friends, rock 'n' roll, Shakespeare, and cats.

https://www.hiraethsffh.com/product-page/whispers-of-magic

A Change in the Contract
Glenis Moore

The minute I regained consciousness I knew that he was stronger than me: arrogant, determined to push me down and live his life in my body. The money he had paid to insert his mind into me would keep my family alive for a while at least but it was all pointless if I could not get back to them, if I could not survive long enough to let them know what I had done and why.

I knew he would be weakened initially by the insertion process so I had up to about twenty minutes until he took over completely. Hence I asked to see the contract again just to check what we had both agreed to. There it was in black and white: insertion of a deceased's mind into a living body upon the payment of £10,000 to the recipient's body. All proceeds to go to the relations of the inserted mind if the process is unsuccessful or the body dies.

There seemed nothing that I could do as, once he took over, I knew that my family would never see that money. But perhaps if I could make just a little change there might be a chance.

I could feel him beginning to take control as we left the Reincarnation Centre. However, I had just enough strength left to throw us under an approaching driverless bus and, as we both died, I smiled to myself knowing that the contract now read: all proceeds to go to the relations of the recipient's body if the process is unsuccessful or if the body dies.

***

Aliens & Others
By G. O. Clark

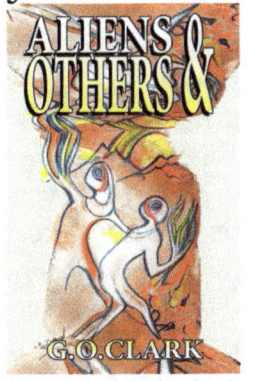

From out of left field, beyond the Pale, farther than stars, nearer than you think. G. O. Clark, telling stories in Bradburyesque fashion, takes you to the odd sides of life, where what you think is real might be an illusion, and what you fear might be real, is.

Type: Collection of short stories.

Ordering links:

Print ($9.00):
https://www.hiraethsffh.com/product-page/aliens-others-by-g-o-clark

PDF ($3.99):
https://www.hiraethsffh.com/product-page/aliens-others-by-g-o-clark-1

Where Did All the Fairy Tale Creatures Go?

Gary Davis

Ricky had been hiking through the big forest near his town all afternoon. He had played in the outskirts of these woods since he was a little kid. Now that he was 13 years old, Ricky liked to take long walks deep into the recesses of the forest. He was hiking along a narrow path that he had never seen before and looked unused for many years.

It was now late afternoon, and Ricky started slowing down; his legs were feeling sore. Before returning home, he wanted to find a place to rest for a few minutes. To his left, he noticed a small clearing. In the center of the clearing, Ricky saw the giant stub of a tree trunk projecting from the ground. It was broad, flat and completely topped with thick, soft green moss. It looked like an inviting place to take a short nap.

Ricky noticed that the clearing was surrounded by a closely-spaced ring of narrow, gnarly oak trees. They were all the same height. These trees were covered in a thick canopy of crimson leaves. That seemed strange for early July; autumn foliage colors wouldn't normally come out for several more months. Ricky could see that all of the trees outside this oak circle sprouted normal green leaves. He didn't see any other clearings in the adjacent woods. He also noticed that none of the red leaves had fallen to the ground. They looked just as healthy and shiny as the surrounding green canopies.

Ricky was getting sleepy, so he sat down and slumped over on the mossy tree stump. He was surprised at how comfortable it felt, almost like his bed at home. Ricky then lay flat on his back and closed his eyes. The temperature was in the upper 80s, but Ricky could feel a cool breeze blowing across his face. This would be the perfect afternoon nap.

Ricky's thoughts quickly drifted to his elderly grandmother, who had passed away only three weeks ago. He had always been close to her. Ricky remembered how his talkative grandmother had read fairy tales to him when he was a little boy—stories like Hansel and Gretel, Goldilocks and the Three Bears, and his favorite, Little Red Riding Hood. His grandmother had both Germanic and Irish ancestors. She was steeped in the myth and lore of ancient Europe.

Ricky's grandmother used to say that the witches and other creatures in old fairy tales had actually existed thousands of years ago. She maintained that the early Europeans, however, had driven them away, deep into the dark woods, perhaps literally. Celts and other groups worshipped spirits that lived inside trees. Druid priests performed sacrifices to appease these spirits. Did the Druid rituals in sacred groves include human sacrifices? No one knows for sure.

Aided by the cool breeze, Ricky fell into a dream-sleep on top of the tree stump. He began dreaming that he was in the middle of a new house. Ricky was sitting on a plush sofa in the living room. The room was built with freshly cut wood and not painted on the inside. The tables in the living room were filled with potted, leafy-red plants.

Ricky dreamed that he was surrounded by other kids about his own age. The kids' mouths were open, but he could not hear what they were saying. It seemed like most of them were laughing or singing. Several were playing games on their smartphones. One red-haired girl was eating chocolate cookies. A boy was bringing Ricky a bag of chips and a bottle of soda.

The kids then stopped what they were doing, moved towards the center of the room and joined hands in a circle around Ricky. They raised and lowered their arms and began walking counterclockwise, or *widdershins*. The kids gradually increased their speed. They appeared to be singing happily although again, Ricky couldn't hear anything. This went on for several minutes.

All of a sudden, the kids stopped in their tracks. They turned their heads from side to side. Ricky could see that something was disturbing them. Their smiles turned into frowns and looks of fear. The kids all turned around with their backs toward Ricky. They began staring anxiously at the rough wooden walls of the living room. The kids thrust their arms out in front of them with the palms up. It appeared to Ricky that the kids were pushing against something that he couldn't see. They were struggling forcefully against something big and invisible.

Swoosh! All of the kids instantly disappeared from the living room, as if they had been ghosts. At the same moment, Ricky woke up, sweating, from his deep dream-sleep. The cool summer breeze was gone, and he inhaled a strong, warm scent of musky oak. The sunlight above him faded to darkness. The final thing that Ricky saw and felt was a circular thicket of heavy, vertical tree limbs rapidly merging together and closing in on him. He was now completely and softly enveloped inside a massive tree. The ancient oak and its shiny canopy of red leaves basked quietly in the late afternoon sunlight, surrounded by a vast green forest.

The last thing that Ricky heard before becoming one with the tree was a faint, mocking voice from way down in the roots: "The better to eat you with, my dear."

See the crimson leaves that never fall,
and the stick-figure branches that never break.
Oh how those gnarly trees grow so tall,
from the souls of children that they take.

End of Term
Matias Travieso-Diaz

Bennu, the bird with a soul of fire, flew to the shrine of Sun God Atum-Ra in Heliopolis and prostrated himself before the unseen deity. It had been a long flight across the sands and the dark waters and Bennu was exhausted, but it was fear more than fatigue that made him drop his wings and shiver in the presence of his master.

"You have summoned me, O Lord, and I have rushed to come before you. What is your command?"

The response from Atum-Ra came out of the air like a burst of thunder that shook the walls of the ancient structure. "You know well what I desire." There was a momentary pause, as if the God allowed Bennu to acknowledge his understanding; but the bird remained in sullen silence. The voice then continued: "You have served me well for five hundred cycles of the seasons, carrying my commands to man and beast and seeing to it that I am properly worshiped throughout creation. You have grown old in my service and now you must come to rest. You will be consumed by my fire, and out of your embers will rise your successor, to continue your mission for yet another term. Make yourself ready to disappear into the eternal void."

"But Lord" countered the bird, finally regaining his voice despite the terror that paralyzed him, "I do not want to burn. If I turn to cinders, I will be gone for good, and there will be nothing left of me."

"Not so," replied the voice of Atum-Ra. "I shall cause a new phoenix to rise from your ashes, fresh and young, identical to you down to the tiniest tail feather, except for his renewed strength and vitality."

"Maybe he will be *like* me, but not *me*. *I* will still be gone. There will be no resurrection for *me*."

"Bennu, how dare you defy the laws that I have set in place to govern the world's existence? Have you forgotten that your duty is to serve at my pleasure for as long as I command it, and not beyond?"

"I know my duty, but I'm not quite ready to discharge it to its ultimate conclusion."

"Why not?"

"Every day I have spent in my service to you has filled me with pleasure. I have watched humans raise tall temples and humble tabernacles in your honor, and witnessed and partaken of the sacrifices that they have offered in their altars to placate you and the other Gods. I have soared through the skies in the soft mornings of spring and the warm summer afternoons. I have eaten the sweet fruits of the earth and drunk its nourishing waters. I have felt the caresses of the breeze, the gentle kisses of the rain. I have endured high winds, crashing thunder, and blinding lightning. I have savored living in all its manifestations.

"My heart still beats strongly in my breast. My feathers are brittle and faded, but they still gleam at the touch of the rays of the sun as I wander aloft. I know the paths I must follow and am familiar with the ways of men and the gentle or fierce disposition of the beasts in the field. Please let me stay around a bit longer!"

The unseen deity spoke again with a stern voice that was a touch less peremptory than before. "What you ask for is not possible. Everything mortal has a destiny that must be fulfilled: a beginning and an end, a course to be completed and ended with nothing to follow it. I will, however, grant you a boon. You may take to the air one last time and fly as long and far as your wings can carry you. When you touch the ground, I will smite you and create a successor from your ashes. He will bring your remains to me and I will hold them next to my throne forever, and that will be your measure of immortality. Fly away, take a last look at the world — and then you must go."

Bennu uttered a grunt that reflected his dismay and inclined his body forward in obeisance. Then, forgetting for one moment his weariness, he rushed out of the temple and rose into the air, experiencing again the gentle touch of the breeze and the sights and sounds of the vast world that opened beneath his body. Alas, fatigue soon returned and, after two or three circles around the human habitations of Heliopolis, the bird began losing altitude and, despite beating his wings feebly, dropped to the ground.

Bennu felt a sudden burst of gratitude for being granted this last flight. Then there was a sharp snap, like a whip being brandished in the air, and the firebird burst into flames and was consumed instantly, leaving only a mound of ashes to mark his passage through the world. There was another snap, and some of the ashes rearranged themselves into the body of a large, beautiful bird with a prominent fiery crest, red, orange and yellow plumage, and bright blue eyes that shone with youthful intensity.

The newly risen phoenix punctured a wound on a nearby myrrh tree to bleed its gum, and shaped the liquid, as it hardened, into a waxy shell. The phoenix gathered the cinders that remained of his predecessor, dropped them into the shell, and flew back to the temple in Heliopolis to deposit the remains before the presence of the sun god.

The new phoenix then withdrew to carry out his duties for the first time, armed with a knowledge and dispatch that were imparted on him by the one left behind. For he retained all the memories of his predecessor, and in so remembering him at every turn, kept him pretty much alive.

Another chapter in the eternal cycle had just started, yet the progression of phoenix deaths and rebirths would continue for as long as the Gods ruled this earth.

Is There a Sign I Should Know?
(after Enya's lyrics)
Tyree Campbell

The ancient temple now almost excavated, the sun almost set, archeologist Therese Jouclard remained behind on the cobble floor while her digmates sought their tents. Like the others, she had noticed the round hole in the center of the floor. Unlike the others, she knew—or thought she knew—why the hole was there. A bit of scraping earlier had removed some black residue that she recognized. Now, alone and prepared, she meant to make use of her knowledge.

Removing a tapered white candle from her carrybag, she knelt down and placed the base in the hole, and sat back. Her dungarees gave her scant comfort against the cold floor. She locked the chill in a dark nook in the back of her mind, where it became ineffectual. Using a long candle match, she slowly touched the flame to the candle wick; the simple act was more devotion than ignition, for she was seeing through the flame another world, one in which she had traveled before. One in which her twin sister Sienne had passed, and passed from, all those years ago.

Even now, though Therese had aged where Sienne had stopped aging, she imagined they looked the same—young and vibrant and so filled with hope for the future. Therese's eyelids began to shutter her eyes. Half-lidded now, her thoughts empty of all sensations save memory, she regressed back in time. Ten years, and twenty, until the time of their eighteenth birthday when, inexplicably, Sienne had laid down and nevermore awakened.

Even now, her breathing slow and deep, Therese could almost see Sienne walking on the other side of the candlelight. Almost, but not quite. There was a shadow, a figure, like the moving statue of an angel. It crossed—or seemed to cross—the temple floor. But it paused to gaze through the flickering light at Therese, as if to say, "If I could be where you are..." A face morphed into the faint orange light—a face on the verge of perpetual tears, of loneliness, with lips trembling as if they fought to hold back the sign of sorrow.

Therese knew that look well, for often over the years she had worn it, and on nights had surrendered to the flood. She murmured back, "If I could be where you are." And while the memory of Sienne watched and waited, Therese laid back on the cold stone floor, and closed her eyes, and presently joined the memory of her twin.

Heir Apparent
Tyree Campbell

Answering a distress call, March and Myrrha find a young woman who has deliberately been marooned on an uninhabited world. She claims to be Hoya Palologa, heir to the Palologa throne on Wanderby. But there is already a Hoya who has been invested as the heir apparent to that throne. Myrrha believes the claim of the Hoya she and March have encountered. Thus begins a journey to establish the succession, a journey made far more perilous because Hoya not only claims the throne, but is also a sinister personage with several crimes on her resume.

March and Myrrha find themselves embroiled in internal politics on Wanderby, where the slightest wrong move can get them killed. The rulers on that world are oblivious to the subtle machinations of their underlings, one of whom has created a lookalike but false Hoya. Which one is which? And will death take the real one before March and Myrrha can stop it?

Type: Novel – science fiction

Ordering Links:
Print: https://www.hiraethsffh.com/product-page/heir-apparent-by-tyree-campbell
PDF: https://www.hiraethsffh.com/product-page/heir-apparent-by-tyree-campbell-2
ePub: https://www.hiraethsffh.com/product-page/heir-apparent-by-tyree-campbell-1

Woman in the Moon
(Dedicated to Delonto Mae Relf)
Terrie Leigh Relf

The seductively sweet scent of oleander entranced and distracted me at the corner of Gramma's house where the magenta, mauve, and pink-tipped flowers bloomed in the moonlight. I touched a delicate petal. When I brought it close to my face to inhale its intoxicating fragrance, Gramma said, "Don't touch the Oleander -- it's poisonous! If you eat it, you'll lose your voice!"

"I'm not going to eat it, Gramma. Just smell it," I protested, amazed, even as a young girl, that something of beauty could be dangerous. I turned away from the flowers, away from the real or imagined threat of muteness.

Even though Gramma constantly reminded me that she was an old woman, she didn't look or seem elderly to me. Her waist-length blue-black hair cascaded down her back and over her shoulders; only a few strands of silver flowed through it.

"Let's walk around the block again," she said. At first, I hesitated, then wanting to please her, agreed.

I squirmed as we walked but she didn't seem to notice. I often wondered why she wanted me to walk with her when she was in one of her reflective moods, but then so much about Gramma was a mystery. "There's a woman in the moon," she said, while I covered my eyes in fear of the cold white light.

"OK, Gramma, there's a woman in the moon." A part of me wanted to believe her -- still wants to believe her -- but I now know that belief, like so many things in life—and death—is an elusive power.

Gramma had powers. Her son, my father, called them "dark." She called them "light." I often felt that there was but a horizon's edge that separated one from the other. "You're a lot like me," Gramma would often say, and then become unusually still.

I shivered, feeling the moon's cold stare as I took one step and then another down the block. Sometimes I would try to count my steps, but I would often become distracted and forget what number I was on. How many steps had I taken with Gramma? Could I ever count that high?

As we neared the next corner, Gramma stopped in front of a familiar house, turned to me, and said, "You remember Lenore, don't you, Lily? This is where she lived," Gramma said, pointing toward a small cottage with an unkempt yard, where flowers lay without their sweet nectar, trampled by a recent rain.

While Gramma was reminiscing aloud, Lenore appeared in the front window, seated in a dark-green velvet chair, a grey Persian cat on her lap, its tail furled around the book she read. Sensing our presence, she set down the book she was reading and rose slightly from her chair in greeting. Her cat leapt gracefully from her lap onto the windowsill, watching us through the window with iridescent eyes.

Passing the next yard, Gramma nodded to a man watering his roses across the street. Their eyes met, rested for a moment, then seemed to part reluctantly. He reminded me of a photograph on Gramma's piano, someone she had known long ago, someone I sensed she loved. I turned around to see if he watched our passage, but he—and his roses—had gone.

As we continued our walk, Gramma occasionally paused in front of someone's house, tilting her head towards it, listening. It was a while, though, before she stopped for longer than a moment or two and spoke.

"And you remember Bernice, don't you dear? How I miss our card games!"

Gramma leaned against the fence in front of Bernice's house. A strand of ivy reached for and clung to her hand. She removed it gently, so as not to break the stem, then sighed, "How I miss my friends."

Out of the corner of my eye, I watched as Bernice appeared the door, holding the screen open just far enough to beckon us inside.

I shivered again, feeling a familiar call, from whom I wasn't sure.

"You should have brought a sweater," Gramma said, as if a sweater's warmth could protect against this penetrating chill.

We came to the empty lot just around the corner from Gramma's house where I had spent so many afternoons alone. I would lie on my back, watch the play of light and shadow through the overhanging branches of the lone Pepper tree. Oftentimes, I would roll the mauve-brown peppercorns between my fingers, imagining that they were magic.

Gramma wanted to walk some more, but this time she wanted to walk towards the ocean. "It's so beautiful at night," she said.

Longing to return to the house but unsure what would happen once we arrived, I shielded my face and eyes from the moon's presence. Gramma pulled my arm down.

"Look!" She pointed at the moon. I felt courageous for a moment, until I noticed how the moon's visage shined full upon me.

Sensing my concern, Gramma said, "Don't worry about it, dear -- she will guide and protect you."

"Who?" I asked, believing then as I do even now that Gramma was the only one who could take care of me, that she had been the one to bring me over when I drowned. I moved closer to her, reached for her hand as we neared the beach. The closer we came to the boardwalk, the tighter I held onto her.

"The grunion are running," someone had said earlier, and I remember wanting to see the silvery bodies undulating in the moonlight, burrowing deep into the sand, their eggs foaming from their bodies like the froth of a wave. Did they really exist, or were they part of someone's dream?

The tides were high due to a sudden storm, but it was low tides that frightened me because they uncovered what was usually hidden.

I watched a wave as it neared shore, thinking how beautifully it swelled and peaked, curving around and under itself. Even as it tugged at my feet and the silvery sand gave way beneath me, I thought of how it would feel to be held in its embrace.

The water was cold, brutally cold, so I imagined that I was a seal playing out beyond the breakers, rolling over and under the surface with each oncoming wave, and then that I was a mischievous mermaid, playing hide-and-seek with my Selkie sisters far out beyond the storm-thrashed breakers.

But I grew tired of my fanciful thoughts and rolled over onto my back to gaze full upon my first Blue Moon. I was in awe of her beauty resonating across the wide expanse of an indigo sky, her hair alight with stars which I traced with an imaginary hand, unable to lift my own. A curious tugging began in my lower abdomen and then a cold heat coursed through me, exploding into a brilliant light. From somewhere far away, I heard a haunting melody, so exquisitely beautiful that my eyes began to tear. I followed the sound and saw an old woman lifting a fragile form from its nest of tangled seaweed fronds and driftwood limbs. She held the child close against her, then leaned back into the water, disappearing from view.

"You're dreaming again," Gramma said, gently shaking my shoulder. I remembered times when she would tuck me into bed at night, pulling the warm flannel sheets up to my chin, followed by a series of multi-colored Afghans that she had crocheted with my Great Grandmother and Great Aunts. Before turning out the light, Gramma would place a rouged kiss upon my forehead and say, "Sweet dreams and no worries—goodnight."

"Don't forget my night-light, Gramma," I would reply.

"The moon will light your way, sweetie," Gramma would always respond.

I wanted to believe that her simple spells would work, that nightmares would vanish once they were remembered, and that the horrors within them were like stars, an intense but faraway light.

But I know differently now.

I awoke in the middle of the night and Gramma was kneeling at the side of my bed whispering something in my ear. When she saw that I was awake, she said, "Go back to sleep, Lily, it's late."

"Then why'd you wake me, Gramma?" I yawned sleepily.

"I just wanted to see you again," she said softly, "before I go."

"OK Gramma, g'night."

In the morning, the aroma of lemon and poppy seed muffins roused me from sleep.

"Good morning, sleepy-head," she smiled as I sat down at the table, watching her smear butter on hot muffins.

"I had the strangest dreams last night, Gramma."

She paused, set down the butter knife, placed her palms together, collecting her thoughts.

"Dreams are like the layers of the onion. When you peel each layer away, there's another and then another, and still another layer," Gramma said.

"But then there's nothing left," I responded, perplexed. But Gramma just smiled at my confusion.

"No, Lily, there's more. So much more."

We continued to eat muffins and sip Earl Grey tea in a comforting silence. After a time Gramma said, "Are you ready to go back now?"

She knew the answer before she asked, but Gramma always said that I had a choice. I knew that my family might miss me. I had a few friends, too, but what I really wanted was to stay with Gramma at her house forever.

"Okay, I'll go back . . . but Gramma?"

"Yes, Lily?"

"I always knew you'd find a way to visit me after you'd gone, but I never thought it would be like this."

Gramma laughed heartily, throwing her head back, nearly losing her balance in the shifting sand.

"Will I ever see you again, Gramma?"

"Perhaps—" her voice trailed off as she turned to search the sky over the horizon's edge, the moon a pale grey in the approaching dawn.

"Let's walk a bit longer, Lily. The living can always wait."

The Sisterhood of the Blood Moon
By Terrie Leigh Relf

For thousands of Earth years, the Transgalactic Consortium has had an invested interest in this planet and its inhabitants, the Haurans. While the Sisterhood of the Blood Moon and the Guardians work together with the Consortium and Haurans to restore balance to the universe, the Blood Moon is fast approaching. The power of this moon reveals untold secrets . . . including the sacred covenant with the Mora Spiders. There is an ancient pact that continues to be honored - but at what cost and for whose purpose?

The world may come to an end. But will there be a chance for a new beginning? And if so, where?

Type: Novel – science fiction/fantasy

Print Edition:
https://www.hiraethsffh.com/product-page/sisterhood-of-the-blood-moon-by-terrie-leigh-relf

Pevely Keiser in:
THE DESERT LARK

Five hundred years into the future, Pevely Keiser is the capo of the criminal organization called Temmen. Temmen runs itself, for the most part, with only a few lethal nudges from Pevely to keep people in line. Lately she has two things on her mind. She wants to do something good and useful with the funds that accrue to the gang. And she wants a companion or two to help her…and perhaps to share her bed, for she well knows it's lonely at the top.

Now she has a chance to snag a billion in cash. But there's a catch: two different planets control the money, and will go to any lengths to see that it is delivered to the right place at the right time. Pevely has help: a ne'er-do-well young man with a checkered past, and a teen-age woman who loves the desert world where the money is now, and who engages in a secret rebellion that could get Pevely killed.

Type: Novel – science fiction adventure
Print: https://www.hiraethsffh.com/product-page/desert-lark-by-tyree-campbell

PDF: https://www.hiraethsffh.com/product-page/desert-lark-by-tyree-campbell-2

Who?

Glenis Moore has been writing flash fiction and poetry since the beginning of the first Covid lockdown. She does most of her writing at night as she suffers from severe insomnia. When she is not writing she makes beaded jewellery, reads, cycles and sometimes runs 10K races slowly. She has been previously published by Infinity Wanderers, Witcraft and CafeLit.

Gary Davis enjoys exercising his imagination through crafting dark stories and poems. He particularly likes classic supernatural horror. Mr. Davis has published about ten short stories in all, mostly in Hiraeth and related predecessor publications. His favorite topics are Halloween and vampires. His most recent stories appear in *The Hungur Chronicles* and explore the connections between vampires, aliens and outer space.

Maureen Bowden is a Liverpudlian, living with her musician husband in North Wales. She has had 193 stories and poems accepted by paying markets and she was nominated for the 2015 international Pushcart Prize. In 2019 Hiraeth Books published an anthology of her stories 'Whispers of Magic' and they plan to publish an anthology of her poems in the near future. She also writes song lyrics, mostly comic political satire, set to traditional melodies. Her husband has performed them in folk music clubs throughout the UK. She loves her family and friends, rock 'n' roll, Shakespeare, and cats.

Terrie Leigh Relf is on staff at Hiraeth Publishing and is honored to have been recently appointed to be the lead editor of *Flash Digest*. She is also the lead editor of *Hungur Chronicles,* the contest judge and editor for the Drabbler Harvest contests, and an editor at large. She is currently revising the third book in her dark sci-fi trilogy, *Beacon Lights of Ranat*.

www.ingramcontent.com/pod-product-compliance
Lightning Source LLC
LaVergne TN
LVHW021953060526
838201LV00049B/1690